The Long and Short Tail of Colo and Ruff

by Diane Lang

illustrated by Laurie Allen Klein

Pounce!

Colo, the cougar cub, just couldn't resist jumping on her mother's tail one more time.

Cougars (Latin name: *Puma concolor*) are also known as mountain lions, panthers, pumas, and catamounts.

Mama Cougar lifted her head. "Leave my tail alone and go find something else to do! Look, there's a feather blowing around. Go play with that."

🐾 Where is papa cougar? Off by himself. Male cats do not help raise their young.

Colo raced off, jumping from rock to rock as gusts of air pushed the feather this way and that.

With each jump, Colo's long tail helped her balance as she almost flew through the air.

🐾 Cougars use their long tails for balance and steering as they leap or run.

As Colo made one more jump, she heard a voice from the grass: "I love how you jump!"

"Who's that?" asked Colo.

"Just me," said the voice. It came from Ruff, a bobcat cub. "You can jump so far, and you don't even get twisted up in the air before you come down. I wish I could do that."

🐾 Bobcats are sometimes called wildcats. Latin name: *Lynx rufus.*

"It's not so hard," said Colo. "I'll do it again, and you can jump with me."

Ruff climbed up on the boulder with Colo. They both crouched and then took off.

Colo made it easily to the next boulder, but
Ruff landed between the two rocks, barely
staying on his feet.

🐾 Cougars have very
powerful rear legs and
are strong climbers.

"I think I see the problem," said Colo. "First of all, you're smaller than I am, so you can't jump as far. But also—you have a very short tail. I think you need a longer tail for balance."

"I sure do," said Ruff. "Yours is so long and beautiful. What's the matter with me?"

"I'm sure nothing is the matter with you. But, you do have an unusual tail."

Colo thought for a moment. "My mom said to go find something to do. Let's go find a new tail for you!"

"Oh," said Ruff. "What a wonderful idea!"

🐾 Bobcats have naturally short tails. "Bobbed" means cut short, although these cats are born that way.

In just a few steps, they saw a lizard. "Look at him," said Ruff. "His tail is long and graceful! Maybe I could use that kind."

As Ruff jumped toward the lizard to get a better look, his paw landed on the end of the lizard's long, slender tail.

What happened next surprised both of the young cats. The tail stayed under Ruff's paw, but the rest of the lizard ran off!

"Look at that!" exclaimed Colo. "That kind of tail breaks off! We'd better look for a different one for you."

🐾 Many lizards are able to drop part of their tail when threatened. It grows back within a few months.

"How about that one?" Ruff had spotted a red-tailed hawk on a nearby branch. "It's a beautiful tail, and I've seen hawks change the shape of their tails while they are flying. I'd love to do that."

🐾 Birds can adjust their tail feathers to the shape they need for fast flight, making turns, or landing.

At that moment, a single feather came loose from the hawk's tail and fell to the ground.

"Uh oh!" cried Ruff. "Her tail is coming apart!"

"How strange," said Colo. "She may be losing just one feather, but you'd better not take any chances. I'm sure a bobcat's tail shouldn't do that."

🐾 Birds lose feathers almost all year long, just one at a time. When a feather on one side drops out, the same feather on the other side will soon be lost. A new feather gradually grows back in.

"How about a fancy one?" Colo asked, as she spotted a skunk in the distance, sporting a beautiful, big, black and white tail.

"It's gorgeous!" exclaimed Ruff. "And so fluffy! Let's go look."

But the beautiful black and white tail was soon high in the air as the skunk sprayed a strong, stinky mist toward the pair of curious cats.

As Ruff and Colo dashed away, Ruff said, "I don't think I want that kind. I need to hide, and I can't hide if I have a smelly tail."

🐾 Some skunks can balance on their front feet and bend their back so that they can spray in the direction they are looking.

A gopher appeared in the nearby grass.

"Look, a gopher! Want to ambush him?" asked Colo.

"Ambush?" asked Ruff. "What does that mean?"

🐾 Cougars and bobcats sometimes
hide and wait for a deer or rabbit or
other prey to go by.

"It means you hide until something passes, and then you pounce on it."

"That sounds fun! And then what do we do with it?"

"I don't know, said Colo. "Mom hasn't told me yet."

🐾 Cats, who only eat meat, must be taught to hunt by their mothers.

Just as they started to move, the gopher quickly turned and disappeared down her hole. The last thing the cats saw was the tip of her tiny tail.

"That gopher was so fast!" exclaimed Ruff. "And you know what else? She had a tail even shorter than mine!"

"Hey!" replied Colo. "Maybe that's why she could turn around so easily!"

🐾 Gophers can turn around in their narrow burrows very rapidly. They can also run backwards and forward in those burrows at equal speed.

"That's it!" said Ruff. "Cougars are strong and run fast, but bobcats have to be quick and agile. Maybe I'm built to move fast through the rocks and the grass, just like my mom. I guess I have a pretty handy tail, after all.

"And speaking of moms," he continued, "I need to go find mine. I'm getting hungry."

Off he ran, his short tail bobbing behind.

🐾 Cats are mammals; the young ones must get milk from their mothers before they are old enough to hunt.

Colo was hungry, too, and as she returned to her mother, she saw that the feather had floated back near their den. She made one more pounce and landed near the large cat once more.

Her mother looked up. "Aren't you clever, Colo," she said, " to be able to entertain yourself with one feather all afternoon long."

For Creative Minds

Cat Comparisons

	cougar	bobcat	house cat
Scientific name	*Puma concolor*	*Lynx rufus*	*Felis catus*
body length (not including tail)	3-6 feet .9-1.8 meters	26-41 inches 66-104 cm	18 inches 46 cm
tail length	25-37 inches 64-94 cm	4-7 inches 10-18 cm	12 inches 30 cm
weight	120-200 lbs 54-91 kg	11-30 lbs 5-14 kg	8-16 lbs 4-7 kg
distance they can jump	20-40 feet 6-12 meters	10 feet 3 meters	8 feet 2.4 meters
lifespan	8-13 years	10-12 years	12-18 years
most active	at dusk and dawn (crepuscular)	at dusk and dawn (crepuscular)	at dusk and dawn (crepuscular)
Is it dangerous to pet?	Yes, you should not approach or try to pet wild animals. They may be scared and try to defend themselves from you.		Depends on the cat! Some like to be petted, some don't.

Cat Maps

There are four types of wildcats in North America. Match each cat map to the description of the cat's habitat and range.

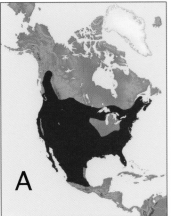

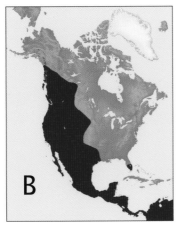

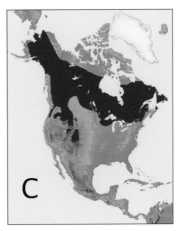

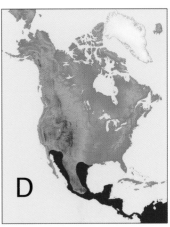

Bobcats live across most of the United States, except for a portion of the Midwest near the Great Lakes. They live in many different types of habitats, like forests, swamps, deserts, and suburban areas near people.

Ocelots live in warm, tropical habitats where there is dense vegetation. Tropical rainforests, grasslands, and marshes are all home to ocelots.

Cougars are mostly found in the western part of North America, although there is one type of cougar found in Florida. Like bobcats, cougars live in many habitats, including swamps, forests, grasslands, and cities. Cougars can also be called mountain lions, pumas, panthers, or catamounts.

Lynxes live in boreal forests in the northern part of North America. Boreal forests are snowy forests of coniferous trees, like pine and spruce.

Which North American wildcat lives mostly in Canada?

Canada

United States of America

Mexico

Are there any regions where cougars and bobcats might meet in the wild? Where?

Which lives mostly in Mexico and Central/South America?

Answers: A-bobcat. B-cougar. C-lynx. D-ocelot.

Tail Adaptations

Adaptations help animals succeed in their habitat. An animal's tail is a type of **physical adaptation**. Different animals can have tails that look very different but serve a similar purpose.

Two of the animals in this book have tails that help them turn. Gophers spin around inside their burrows. Bobcats change directions as they dart through rocks and grass.

Two of the animals in this book have tails that help them balance. Cougars use their long tails to balance as they leap. Hawks use their winged tails to balance and steer as they soar through the air.

Two of the animals in this book have tails that help them defend themselves. Skunks raise their tails to spray predators. Lizards' tails come off when a predator grabs them, allowing the lizard to escape.

Can you think of any other animals that use their tails to turn, balance, or defend themselves? Can you think of other uses for tails?

An animal's physical adaptations can tell you something about the animal and the habitat it lives in. Match the adaptations below with how it helps the animal.

Can you think of any animals that have these adaptations?

1. thick fur
2. webbed toes
3. sharp teeth
4. hard outer shell
5. whiskers

A. sense things near its face
B. stay warm in cold habitats
C. protect itself from attack
D. paddle through wet habitats
E. tear through meat

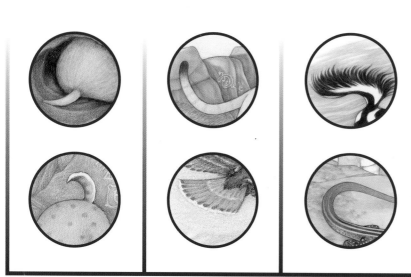

turn   balance   defense

Do you have a tail? If you had a tail, what type of tail would you want?

Answers: 1B, 2D, 3E, 4C, 5A

Match the Tail

A

B

C

D

E

F

cougar

gopher

hawk

lizard

bobcat

skunk

Answers: A-skunk, B-hawk, C-bobcat, D-gopher, E-cougar, F-lizard

For Patti Blasquez, whose love of wildlife helped open my eyes to every creature, large and small— DL

Thanks to Tiffany Dollins and Hardy Kern, Animal Program Specialists at the Columbus Zoo for ensuring the accuracy of the information in this book.

Library of Congress Cataloging-in-Publication Data

Names: Lang, Diane, author. | Klein, Laurie Allen, illustrator.
Title: The long and short tale of Colo and Ruff / by Diane Lang ; illustrated
  by Laurie Allen Klein.
Description: Mt. Pleasant, SC : Arbordale Publishing, [2019] | Audience:
  Grades K-3. | Audience: Ages 3-7. | Includes bibliographical references.
Identifiers: LCCN 2018040513 (print) | LCCN 2018049538 (ebook) | ISBN
  9781607187561 (English ebook PDF) | ISBN 9781643511566 (English ePub3) |
  ISBN 9781607187684 (Interactive, read-aloud ebook features selectable
  English) | ISBN 9781607187387 (English hardcover) | ISBN 9781607187448
  (English paperback) | ISBN 9781607187493 (Spanish paperback) | ISBN
  9781607187622 (Spanish ebook PDF) | ISBN 9781643513140 (Spanish ePub3) |
  ISBN 9781607187745 (Interactive, read-aloud ebook features selectable
  Spanish)
Subjects: LCSH: Tail--Juvenile literature.
Classification: LCC QL950.6 (ebook) | LCC QL950.6 .L36 2019 (print) | DDC
  591.47--dc23
LC record available at https://lccn.loc.gov/2018040513

Lexile® Level: 650L
Keyword phrases: animal adaptations, physical adaptations, tails

Bibliography/ Bibliografía-:

Bobcat Fact Sheet. Arizona Sonora Desert Museum. Internet. 2, 2016
Big Cats Wild Cats. Internet. 2, 2016
Corrigan, Patricia, "Cougars," in "Our Wild World" series, NorthWood Press, 2001
Halfmann, Janet. *Little Skink's Tail*. Mt. Pleasant, SC: Arbordale Publishing (formerly Sylvan Dell), 2007. Print.
Hodge, Deborah, "Wild Cats: Cougars, Bobcats and Lynx," Kids Can Press Wildlife Series, 1996
Holland, Mary. Animal Tails. Mt. Pleasant, SC: Arbordale Publishing, 2017. Print
Frequently Asked Questions. Mountain Lion Foundation. Internet. 2, 2016
Squire, Ann O., "Bobcats"; True Books: Animals, Children's Press, 2005

Manufactured in China, December 2018
This product conforms to CPSIA 2008
First Printing

Arbordale Publishing
Mt. Pleasant, SC 29464
www.ArbordalePublishing.com